The DREAM TRAVELER'S QUEST

-3-
THE GARDEN AND THE SERPENT

TED DEKKER
KARA DEKKER

Theo stood in the back of the classroom, leaning against the wall, flipping through his latest edition of *The Vanisher*. The overhead bell would announce the beginning of a new school day at any moment.

He turned to the next page, one eye on the ticking second hand of the classroom clock. Each new day was another opportunity for his next quest to begin. It had been more than a week since he and Annelee had been to other earth. Waiting for the next quest was making him anxious, nervous, worried, and a bit stir-crazy.

Two seals—three to go. Then what?

He didn't know. But with each seal his world was changing—not in a small way, either. It was almost as if he was becoming a new person—not actually a new person but more like he was discovering a part of himself that he had forgotten existed.

The bell rang. Theo blinked away his thoughts. He stuffed his comic book in the back pocket of his backpack, took his normal seat—last row, second chair—and waited for the other students to enter and settle.

"Ready for another school day, Theo?" Mrs. Baily asked as she wrote the day's language arts lesson on the board. *Point of View: Andrew Jackson*.

"Yup."

Honestly, he would rather be running around with three white bats in other earth.

His classmates entered and took their seats. He nibbled at his lip as he watched the door, waiting for Annelee to enter the room.

He heard her laugh in the hallway. Butterflies fluttered in his belly. Annelee turned into the class with a giant smile on her face, surrounded by friends.

She'd been so different since they'd returned from other earth. She smiled more, laughed more, and talked to everyone, not just her usual group of girlfriends. She even swore off her teen beauty magazines for reasons she said Theo wouldn't understand—something about make-up and trying to look like photo-shopped puppies. Maybe she had said *puppets*. Or people. Whatever she had said, discovering her true beauty had changed her.

She bounced over to Theo and took the seat next to him.

"Any signs yet, dream traveler?"

Dream traveler. He liked the way that sounded, and he loved having a friend to share his secret. Especially since it was Annelee. He didn't know who would go with him next, but no one could match Annelee.

"No, nothing yet."

"I want to go back to other earth so bad! How do you think Maya's doing? Are you sure you haven't heard anything? You'd tell me, wouldn't you?"

Even though a lot had changed about Annelee, she still asked a lot of questions. But he didn't mind.

"Of course I'd tell you. But keep it down. People will start to think you've lost it if they hear you talking about other worlds and dream traveling."

Annelee rolled her eyes and gave Theo a small shove. "Who cares what they think. I'm the light of the world, remember?"

Theo laughed. Sometimes he wondered if Annelee understood who she was in Elyon better than he did, but that didn't bother him. Her enthusiasm was infectious.

"How long did it take them to come back last time? Two weeks?"

"About that," he said.

"So it could be any day. I don't think I can wait any longer."

Mrs. Baily's voice rang out over the room of sixth-graders. "All right, class! Time to start. Quiet, please." As if on queue, the bell rang once more, announcing the start of first period.

The room quieted down. Mrs. Baily began her lesson on writing from the point of view of Andrew Jackson, America's seventh president. Theo tried to listen but was too distracted. Not only had he had about enough of the crossover lessons between sixth-period American history and first-period language arts, but his thoughts were consumed with other earth.

Who could be coming with me this time?

His eyes scanned the room, thinking through each student, but none of them seemed like a good fit. Then again, neither had Annelee. He'd hardly known her.

Regardless, one thing was certain: they would be in for a surprise. Each time he'd gone to other earth, something terrible had happened that had turned into something amazing. He had to remember that the next time.

If the next time ever comes.

But still . . . he'd been in some seriously dangerous situations. Fighting off Shataiki bats, thrown in a dungeon, tied to a post—Talya said that the next quest would be even harder. What if it all went bad? What if he got seriously hurt, lost an arm, suffered a major head wound, or worse? He didn't think there was a section in the *Home Medical Reference Guide* for dismemberment by Shataiki.

"Hi, Theo," a voice said by the classroom door.

He knew that voice! He jerked his head up. There in the doorway stood Michal with Stokes, grinning.

"Surprise," Stokes said, wobbling in.

"Stokes!" Annelee's voice squeaked.

Mrs. Baily turned around. "Did someone have a question about point of view?"

Theo glanced at the Roush, then back at the teacher, reminding himself that only he and Annelee could see things from other earth.

"Um, Annelee sneezed!" he said louder than he had intended.

Annelee picked up the hint and "sneezed" again. "St-o-kes!"

"Bless you!" Mrs. Baily turned back to the board, dry-erase marker in hand.

He looked over at Annelee with his finger held to his lips. "Shhh!"

"Right," she mouthed. He turned his attention back to his furry friends and winked. He was so excited to see those big green eyes, fluffy bodies, and crazy smiles.

Michal waddled in and jumped onto Mrs. Baily's desk with his wings on his hips. He looked as if he could've been teaching the class. It would make sense, after all. He was actually a teacher—a supreme teacher of a whole different kind. If the other students could see him, they would flip out.

Stokes leaped into the air, flew across the room, and landed squarely on Theo's desk. He wrapped his wings around Theo's shoulders, hugging too tight.

Theo replaced the urge to laugh with a cough and almost returned the hug. But then he remembered where he was. The other students would definitely think he'd lost it if they saw him hugging the air.

Stokes hopped over to Annelee and threw his wings around her. She hugged him back. But then she caught herself, shrugged, and sat back as if nothing had happened. This was part of the new Annelee— the part that didn't care that Betty Ringwald was now staring at her with her mouth half open.

Michal cleared his throat. "If you don't mind, Stokes. You're being disruptive. Didn't I warn you about this?"

"Sorry," Stokes apologized. He took to the air and joined Michal at the desk where he plopped down on his rump, tiny feet dangling over the edge.

Michal nodded at Theo and Annelee. "It is good to see you again, my friends. No need to respond. Just listen."

Theo smiled. Seeing the Roush made him crave other earth even more.

"It's time," Michal said. "Talya's given us the name of the one who will journey with you. But first," he lifted a finger into the air, "let's talk about what you've learned so far."

Michal plucked a marker from the desk, flew over to the whiteboard, landed on the bottom ledge, and drew a number "1" on the board.

Theo quickly looked to the students on his left and right. No reaction. They couldn't see the number!

"Don't worry, Theo," Stokes said. "Michal is much wiser than me. He knows how to move things without others seeing. Plus, we can hear your thoughts this time. Talya taught us how to do that. He gave us a special fruit, but it only lasts for a little bit, so we must hurry."

They can hear my thoughts?

"Yes, we can," Michal said. "Now as I was saying—"

Annelee turned to Theo and mouthed, "So cool!"

"I know!" Stokes interrupted, digging into his bag. "I have an idea! They can eat some too!"

"Whatever for?" Michal demanded.

"So they can hear each other's thoughts!"

Before Michal could offer an opinion on the matter, Stokes was across the room, handing a round yellow fruit to Annelee.

"Bite it!"

Annelee took the fruit. "Eat this?"

"Eat what?" Betty Ringwald whispered.

Stokes smiled.

Annelee took an exaggerated bite, eyeing Betty playfully.

"Weirdo." Betty rolled her eyes and returned her focus to Mrs. Baily.

Before Annelee could take another bite, Stokes snatched it away and shoved it at Theo, eyes bright. "Bite it!"

Theo took a bite. The fruit was sweet and the juice warm. He blinked and looked at Annelee.

Can you hear me?

Yep. Theo heard Annelee's voice in his head, but her lips weren't moving. The fruit worked!

"Yep!" Stokes said. "What did I say? A brilliant idea, I don't mind saying so myself." And then he flew back to the front of the classroom, plopped down, and grinned at them, obviously satisfied with himself.

So . . .who's coming with me this time? Theo thought, trying out his new ability.

Michal looked at him. "We'll get to that, but first we remember."

This is so cool! I'm like Professor X from the X-Men!

"So cool!" Annelee breathed. Then thought, *It really is like being an X-man!*

"What's an X-man?" Stokes asked.

He's kind of like a superhero genius! He can hear people's thoughts anywhere in world, Theo explained.

"I want to be an X-man too!"

"Silence!" Michal said, frowning at Stokes. "All of you. Focus on me and try not to think."

Stokes smiled sheepishly. Theo tried not to think.

Michal lifted his eyes to Theo. "You learned on your first quest that Elyon is the light and nothing can hurt him, right?"

Right.

Michal wrote the word "light" above the number "1." Then he wrote number "2" next to it. "On your second quest, you both learned that you're the light of the world."

Right, Annelee thought.

"Good." Michal wrote the word "light" above the "2." He then wrote number "3" next to it, dropped the dry-erase marker in the tray, and hopped over to the desk next to Stokes.

"On your third mission you'll begin by discovering that although you're the light of the world, you're still blind to who you are as that light. To this end, you will bring someone very special to help you understand this idea better."

Who? Theo asked, sitting on the edge of his seat.

He had wanted to know the answer to this question for weeks.

Stokes jumped into the air, flew across the room, and landed on the desk of Danny Peters.

"Him!" Stokes announced, finger thrust in Danny's face. "This one!"

Danny? But . . . but he's blind, Theo thought.

"Exactly," Michal said. "And he's going to teach you how important seeing beyond your natural eyes really is."

"How?" Theo asked.

Mrs. Baily turned to face him. "How? What do you mean, Theo? Do I need to go over it again?"

"Sorry, I was just thinking aloud."

She raised an eyebrow and then returned to her teaching. His dad would hear about this.

Michal flew over to Annelee's desk. "As you know, my dear, this new mission will only be for Danny and Theo. But you will have an important role to play."

I will? she asked.

"But of course. You will watch over them as they dream."

"In case something goes wrong!" Stokes blurted from Danny's desk.

Wrong? Theo thought. *Like what?*

"Pay him no mind," Michal said, drilling his furry

friend with a glare. "There is always danger, but I'm sure you can handle it."

He faced Annelee. "Watch over them, and if anything goes wrong, you'll know what to do."

She will? Theo sure hoped she would know what to do.

Annelee crossed her arms matter-of-factly. *Of course I will! I'm the light, remember?*

The Roush nodded, satisfied.

Theo glanced up at Danny, but all he could see was the back of his head and his curly black hair. He leaned to his right. Danny was reading, fingers on a Braille edition of their sixth-grade literature book.

How is a boy with no sight going to help me see?

Michal reached into his satchel and pulled out two red fruits, one of which he tossed to Stokes.

"Goodbye, young ones. Until we see you again." Michal took a bite of his fruit and immediately vanished.

"I will see you soon, son of Dunnery," Stokes said, biting into the fruit. Then he too was gone.

Theo looked at Annelee. *Can you still hear me?*

She didn't respond. He'd take that as a no.

The moment the bell rang, they both jumped to their feet. Mrs. Baily tried to say a few last things about their writing assignment as the rest of the class rose from their seats. Theo watched Danny get up and out of his chair, then use his red-and-white tipped cane to walk down the aisle toward the door. Theo thought about calling after him, but it wasn't the time or place.

"Well, what do we do?" Annelee whispered, coming up beside him.

"We get him to the library. It's our only option."

"How are we going to get him there?" Annelee asked after Danny had left the room.

"The same way I got you there. Ask."

"And when do you plan to ask, smarty pants?"

"Now. I know exactly where to find him. Meet me outside."

Theo found Annelee waiting for him at the old swing set outside the double doors, eating her usual—ham and Swiss cheese on rye. She swung only so slightly as she watched her toes drag against the wood chips, but she quickly found Theo's eyes and waved him over.

She jumped off the swing as he approached. "What took you so long?"

"Had to grab lunch from my dad. But I'm not hungry. Who can eat lunch at ten o'clock in the morning? I just ate breakfast like an hour ago."

"Mom says the cafeteria should be ready next week." She took another bite and swallowed.

"That's what the school board said last week."

She shrugged. "So where's Danny?"

"The old wooden playground. It's where I used

to eat lunch before we . . . I mean, you and I . . . you know, the other earth." He blushed. "He'll be there. He's always there."

"Really? I had no idea anyone still hung out on that old thing. Aren't they tearing it down soon?"

"I think so, along with the rest of the playground." Theo shrugged. "Sad, it's a great hiding spot."

"*Was* a great hiding spot," Annelee winked.

"Right. Was."

She tugged at the sleeve of his coat. "Let's find Danny."

Theo and Annelee maneuvered around the students huddled together in groups, eating their bagged lunches. Theo purposefully looked to his left, avoiding Mr. Grauberger's monitoring eyes on his right. Any lunch monitor was better than The Grauberger, who took delight in keeping the students silent.

"There's a platform between the monkey bars and the slide. He should be there," Theo whispered.

As they approached, he could see Danny leaning up against the wooden wall. Alone.

On tiptoes, Annelee peered over the edge of the dry rotted wood. "Danny?"

"Hmmm?" a voice replied.

"Can you come down here?"

"What for?"

"We need to talk to you."

No answer.

Annelee leaned over again. "Danny? It's okay, we—"

"What about?" Danny asked, suddenly standing behind them with his cane in one hand and a crumbled paper sack in the other. Annelee jumped. Theo spun around.

"Sorry, didn't mean to scare you." Danny Peters appeared to be looking straight at them through his stylish dark glasses.

"No, you're fine," Annelee said. "I'm—"

"Annelee White," Danny said before Annelee could finish.

"How could you tell?"

"Your voice. I hear it in class." Danny turned to Theo. "And Theo Dunnery."

"How did you know it was me?" Theo asked. "I didn't say anything."

"You smell like Band-Aids." He laughed.

Theo was amazed. He never considered that Danny might know every kid in the school by the way they spoke and smelled. Nor had he considered that he smelled like a Band-Aid. But it made sense. His dad was a bit obsessed with the sticky bandages.

"That's incredible!" Annelee said, leaning up against the wooden post. "So, what do I smell like?"

"Like strawberries."

Annelee did smell like strawberries. It was one of the many things Theo loved about her.

"That's my lip gloss!" she said excitedly.

"I know that too," Danny said.

In elementary school, Theo had spent nearly every day of recess hiding with Danny. Even in his first few months of middle school, he and Danny had silently hung out in this very location. But Theo had never known that Danny had this ability.

"So how long have you two been friends?" Danny asked.

"It's a new thing," Annelee said with a smile at Theo.

"Oh. That's why Theo hasn't been around much lately?"

Theo scratched the back of his head. "Sorry about that. I guess I didn't think you noticed."

"No big deal. So, what do you want?"

"Well, we have something kind of weird to ask you. You see, we . . . Annelee and I . . ." Theo paused. "Alright, I'm just going to say it, and I won't blame you if you think we're crazy. Annelee and I travel to a dream world through a book. Every time I go over to this world, a man named Talya tells me I'm gonna bring someone new with me the next time I travel over, and this time he told me it was you."

Theo waited for Danny to start laughing or take the remains of his lunch and leave, but Danny's lips turned upward into a soft smile.

"Sure. I go to dream worlds all the time."

"You do?"

"Don't we all? I mean . . . I practically live in one."

"Theo's telling the truth," Annelee said. "It's a real world, not something in our head. I've been there too, through the book."

"A book, huh?"

"Yup." Annelee glanced at Theo, slightly frustrated. Danny obviously wasn't taking them seriously.

"She's right," he said. "Let us just show you the book. Please . . . you have to come with me."

"What for?"

"I don't know yet. But the Roush said to bring you."

"Roush?" Danny asked.

"Fuzzy white bats." It sounded ridiculous, so Theo changed the subject. "Never mind. You'll see for yourself if you come with us."

"I'm blind, remember? I can't see anything."

"Right." Theo shifted on his feet. "I didn't mean to offend—"

"I'm not offended. I was just kidding!"

"So, does that mean you'll come with us?"

"Sure, okay," Danny said.

"Okay?"

"Yup. Okay."

"Really?"

Danny shrugged. "What can I say? I've always wanted to be a part of a superhero, sci-fi kind of adventure. Besides, I've always known there was something else out there. My dad was a big believer in the unknown . . . before he died. I guess I took after him. So, why not?"

Theo felt bad for Danny but not because he was blind. He remembered the year Danny arrived—third grade. He was the first blind kid Theo had ever seen. The way Danny moved down the hall with ease fascinated him. When Theo got home that afternoon and told his dad about Danny, his dad told him the rest of Danny's story. Danny had no family to take care of him. He'd bounced between foster families for two years until one of the eighth-grade teachers at Whitmore Christian Middle took him into foster care until a more permanent arrangement could be made. As far as Theo knew, Danny still lived with the same teacher.

"So, are we waiting on someone else or are you going to show me this book?"

"No one else," Theo said a bit more excitedly. "Follow us."

Annelee touched Danny on the elbow. "I'll lead you."

"It's okay," he said, pulling his arm free and extending his cane out in front of him. "I'll follow."

Theo led them back through the yard, into the school, and down the hall. "Am I going too fast?"

"Nope. I can hear your steps."

Amazing!

"So, where are we going?" Danny asked.

"The library," Annelee said.

"Right. The book. Makes sense."

"I have a joke for you," a voice bellowed from behind them.

A chill ran down Theo's back. Asher! He turned to see Asher leaning against one of the lockers, sneering. The bully was alone this time, but that didn't mean he couldn't destroy all three of them.

"A blind kid, a wimp, and an ugly girl walk into a school hallway . . . Oh, wait. That's already funny without a punch line!" He clutched his waist and bent over, cackling.

"What do you want, Asher?" Annelee asked, hands balled into fists.

"Never seen you three together before. Just want to know why you are all of a sudden friends. Besides being losers. Seems fishy to me."

"We're going to the library . . . book report," Theo said, thinking it was kind of true. He didn't wait for Asher to respond. He turned and began to walk again with Danny and Annelee close behind.

"Book report, huh?" Asher was following behind. "I didn't hear anything about a stupid book report. I think you're lying. Do you know what I do to liars?" He pounded his fist into the palm of his other hand.

"We're in a different grade, Asher," Annelee said.

"So?" Asher wasn't picking up what she was trying to say.

"We have different teachers! Different assignments? Never mind, just leave us alone."

Asher grabbed her by the shoulder and twisted her around, knocking Danny aside. "It's not nice to be rude, troll!"

Theo spun to face Asher, afraid but unwilling to let the thug mess with Annelee. "Leave her alone!"

"What's going on down there?" a welcomed voice from the end of the hall called to them—Mr. O'Brian, their art teacher.

Asher glanced at Danny and evidently thought better of being caught beating up a girl and a boy with a cane. He released Annelee and backed away from them.

"Fine. Go do your stupid report. But don't think you're off the hook." Asher smirked and then slowly walked away, whistling.

"Let's go," Theo said.

He tried to force Asher from his mind as he pushed open the library doors.

I am the son of Elyon. Nothing can threaten him. I am the light of the world . . .

"Well, well. Looks like this little group is growing." Mrs. Friend sat in her usual spot behind the circulation desk.

"Yep!" Annelee said cheerfully.

Theo leaned slightly into the desk. "Can we—"

"Take Danny to the room?" Mrs. Friend asked,

holding up the key. "Absolutely. Perfect choice. I hope you're learning everything you need to know." She winked.

She knows. She has to know.

He smiled. "We are."

This time Danny let Annelee guide him as they followed Theo up the steps and to the small door. Theo couldn't help the feeling that Danny was going to be more of a burden than a help on this quest. How could Danny help if he couldn't see?

He unlocked the door and walked into the dusty room. It was like it always was—dim, musty, and safe. He flipped on the light switch and breathed in the scent of old leather.

Annelee let go of Danny's elbow and ran to get the book.

"Maybe you should tell Danny more about other earth," Annelee said with the book securely in her arms.

"Other earth?" Danny asked under his breath.

"It's what we call it. I've been twice—once alone and once with Annelee," Theo said.

Danny was silent. For a moment Theo thought he might be having second thoughts. Then he spoke up. "What do you mean you've been there twice? You mean *dreamed* of it twice."

"No, I mean we actually go. Well, I guess it's like a dream, but it's also real. We have to be there to go on the quest to get the seals."

"Seals?" Danny asked. "You mean like the animal?"

"No." Theo laughed. The same thought had crossed his mind when he first heard about the seals. "There are five Seals of Truth. I've already found the first two."

"Seals of truth?"

"They're like lessons we learn. And they show up on our arms. You'll see."

This was the most he and Danny had spoken in all the years they had known one another.

"So, this whole seal thing, seems kinda weird—going into a dream to learn a lesson."

Annelee cleared her throat. "Weird maybe, but it's real. The first lesson was about knowing that Elyon is the light. The second one was about knowing that we are the light. I guess you're going to find out what the third one is. Something about being blind to the light, I think."

It was what Michal had said: "You're still blind to who you are as the light."

Danny frowned. "Interesting. Confusing. But I can definitely help you with the blind part." He turned his face toward Theo before Theo could respond. "Joking! So what do we do?"

Theo was amazed by how willing and laid-back Danny was acting. Maybe he *would* be helpful.

Annelee plopped the book on the floor and pulled Danny down next to her. Theo knelt beside them, looking at the book. He exhaled and tried to calm his hammering heart.

"You have to put a drop of your blood into this book, and then it will take you over," Annelee said. "Theo tricked me into giving my blood last time." She elbowed him playfully. "Poked me with a thumbtack!"

"The blood is like a key," Theo said, ignoring Annelee's comment.

Danny reached forward and gently ran his hand over the book. "You're serious?" By the tightness in his voice, Theo knew Danny was taking them seriously, maybe for the first time. "You actually need my blood?"

"It's the only way. It already has my blood, but it needs yours. I know it sounds ridiculous, but it really does—"

"Do you have something to stick me with?"

The boy is brave, that's for sure, Theo thought, digging a thumbtack he'd taken from the classroom out of his pocket. Maybe that was why Talya had chosen him.

Theo placed the thumbtack into Danny's hand. "Just a tiny prick."

"So prick my finger and put it on this book?" Danny asked.

"Just a small prick," Annelee said, breathing with anticipation.

"What about you?"

"Me? I'm staying here to watch over you while you're gone."

"How can you watch over us if we're gone?"

"We go, but our bodies stay here," she explained.

"How's that?"

"We fall asleep," Theo said. "I think, anyway."

Danny sat unmoving for a few minutes and then lifted the thumbtack.

Excitement filled Theo as he watched Danny poke his fingertip. A drop of red blood bubbled from the prick. He reached out, took Danny's hand, and pressed it on the page under the smudge of his own dried blood.

The book began to glow.

"Are you ready?"

"I feel warmth, but it doesn't smell hot." Danny held his hands over the book like one would over a fire. "And there's a sound, like a ringing. What's happening?"

The room flooded with light. Annelee backed to the corner as she watched the two boys become encircled by the warm glow.

"Be careful, Theo!" she yelled over the hum of the light. "Don't let anything happen to Danny! Remember not to—"

Theo lost the rest of what she was saying. The room faded from sight. And then they were gone.

Theo's eyes popped open. He found himself lying on the ground, surrounded by beautiful green trees.

Where's the desert? Where am I?

The light broke through the leaves, shadows danced around him, and the sun warmed his skin. He breathed in the familiar sweet air. He was back!

"Theo?" Danny's panicked voice cut into his thoughts.

Theo shoved himself up and twisted to see Danny frantically looking around the clearing. His lips were trembling and tears dripped from under the rims of his glasses.

This was not the reaction Theo expected from the boy who had so willingly agreed to come along.

"It's okay! We're in the other earth. I know it's weird, but—"

"It's not that!" Danny cried, removing his glasses. "I . . . I can see!"

Theo jumped to his feet. "You can see?"

"I can see," Danny said, brushing his hand against the grass under him. He picked a blade and twisted it in front of his eyes. "Green. Is this the color green?"

"Yes!"

Danny looked at his hands and smiled. Joyful tears continued to roll down his cheeks. He laughed. "My skin, it's so much darker than yours!"

He rose to his feet and turned in circles, taking in the forest, the flowers, and the streams of light that filtered through the branches. He ran to one of the trees, closed his eyes, and felt the bark. "A tree!"

He caught a leaf as it fell and held it up in the air. "A leaf? What color?"

"Yellow."

"Yellow," Danny breathed. He threw the leaf back into the air. "I love this color!"

Theo hadn't thought much about the color of things. The grass was green, the leaf yellow. It was his normal. But now he really thought to look at it all—the colors, the shapes, the textures.

His new friend ran around the clearing, touching everything from flowers to rocks. He had known them by touch, sound and smell, but now he was learning them by sight.

Danny plopped on the grass, eyes glued to the sky in wonder. "So that's what it looks like. I've always wanted to know. A big burning star, a ball of light."

Theo joined Danny on the grass, squinting up at the sun. He had seen the sun his whole life, but now he looked at it as if he was seeing it too for the first time.

"It's incredible," Danny whispered.

"Yep, incredible. I guess I haven't really looked at it in a while."

"Are you serious? How could you not look at it every day?"

"Theo!" A voice echoed across the clearing. Theo sat up to see Gabil crashing through the tops of the trees.

"What's that?" Danny asked, fumbling to his feet.

Gabil flew into Theo and flung his wings around him. "It is so nice to see you again!"

Michal and Stokes sailed in and landed next to Gabil.

Danny stared at the three giant bats, eyes wide and mouth open. "What are you?"

"So, I see that your eyes are working over here," Michal said. "Talya said that might happen."

"We are Roush," Stokes said, stepping forward and offering a winged hand to shake. "And I am Theo's protector, the Shataiki Slayer."

"Whatever you are, you're so cool!" Danny said, shaking Stokes's hand. Then, "What are Shataiki?"

Theo shivered at the thought. "Like the Roush only they're black with fangs . . . and they're evil."

Gabil grabbed Danny's hand and shook it, not to be outdone by Stokes. "I am Gabil, and that serious-looking one over there is Michal."

Michal ignored the comment and offered a small bow. "It's a pleasure to meet you, Danny." He waddled forward. "And I don't mean to interrupt your discovery of our world, but as always, time is of the essence."

"Time for what?" Danny asked.

"Our quest for the third seal," Theo said. "Like I was telling you about in the library."

"Right. Seals like truths," Danny said. "Not like animals. And quest, not a dream. But I'm asleep." He turned to Michal. "Right? I mean . . . this isn't just a dream. Or is it?"

"I can assure you that I am not a dream—depending on what you mean by dream, that is."

"Okay, so not a dream. Then how will we get back? Wake up?"

"We could, I guess . . . but not until we find the third seal," Theo said.

Danny nodded. "Where do we start?"

"I'm guessing Talya's waiting for us at the top of the mountain, ready to show us the next door." Theo looked around. "But this is different. I don't know where we are."

"Right next to Mount Veritas," Gabil said. "The book dropped you closer this time."

Theo faced Danny. "The book usually drops me off in the middle of a hot desert."

"A desert? Does this place have oceans?"

"This place is the same as Earth," Michal said.

Danny seemed intrigued by that, but he didn't press with more questions.

"Is this world dangerous?" Danny asked.

"Oh yes!" Stokes cried, hopping high. "But that's where I come in! Never fear!" He swiped at the air with his spindly leg. "Stokes is near."

Danny smiled, still a bit uncertain. "Well, okay then."

"Okay then." Theo nodded. "Lead us on, Stokes."

Ten minutes later they were climbing, answering an endless stream of questions from Danny who stopped every few minutes to examine a bush, or a rock, or a butterfly—anything and everything within his sight. Theo didn't mind. He would have done the same thing if he had been blind since birth.

With such slow going, it took them over an hour to reach the huge double doors that would lead them into the mountain.

"Doors on a mountain?" Danny exclaimed.

"You haven't seen anything yet," Theo said, hurrying through the doors, eager to see Talya again.

Midway through the lit passageway, Danny stopped, mesmerized by the burning torches lining the rock walls. "Fire!"

"Come on! There's so much for you to see. I can't wait to show you what's next."

They found Talya in the large open cavern next to the third of the five doors. As always, he was dressed in his long robe, waiting patiently, staff in hand.

Talya lifted an eyebrow. "Well then, you've made it back. And you've succeeded in bringing Danny with you." He studied Danny, who approached him with wide eyes. "And you, young man, are clearly seeing the world in a whole new light."

"I . . ." Danny blinked. "I am."

Talya smiled. "You may call me Talya. Think of me as the master of ceremonies. I will guide you to the quest at hand beyond the third door." He pointed at the door with a solid black circle above it.

"Yes, sir." Danny bowed his head.

"No need for formalities. You may call me Talya."

"You're the one who told Theo to bring me through the book?"

"I did."

"Thank you."

Talya placed his hand on Danny's shoulder. "You are most welcome, young man. But I warn you, you might not always be quite so thankful."

"What do you mean?"

"I mean, seeing the truth can sometimes be more challenging than you might think."

"But I *can* see."

"With your eyes," Talya said, pointing to his own blue eyes, "but can you see the truth?" He tapped his heart. "Time will tell."

"What I think he means is that we have to see differently if we want to find the third seal," Theo said, concerned Talya's somber tone might discourage Danny. "Right?"

"Close enough."

Theo had been through two doors already, and he was ready to enter the third. What waited for them? The waters of Elyon? New friends like Maya?

But the first had also brought Shataiki, and the second had brought Shadow Man. Could there be worse than that? Talya had said the third seal would be harder than the first two.

He had to remember that something good always came out of the bad when he discovered a seal.

Theo looked into Talya's warm eyes and felt his nerves calm. He cleared his throat. "I think we're ready."

"So we're going through one of those doors?" Danny asked.

"But of course you are."

"And so am I!" Stokes's voice squeaked from behind them.

Talya turned to the fluffy friends and smiled. "Indeed you are, little Stokes. And only you. I have another mission for you, Gabil and Michal."

"Yes, sir," Gabil said. Michal gave a strong head

nod.

Stokes yelped in delight, flying over to Danny and Theo. "Never fear! I'll make it easy for you."

Talya cleared his throat, dismissing the young Roush. "Remember this: There are many lenses we see through. Find the right lenses and you'll no longer be blind."

Lenses?

The two torches next to the third door came to life. The big black circle above the door glistened in the flames' light. Danny's eyes grew wide.

"Are you ready?" Talya asked.

Danny nodded. "I think so."

"Remember your training, Stokes," Gabil said.

"But of course!" Stokes led Theo and Danny to the door. As they approached, the door swung open, flooding the room with a bright light. Danny shielded his eyes.

Suddenly, Theo wasn't ready. It was what Talya had said about the lenses. He didn't understand. He needed to know more about the lenses. But before he could ask, fingers of light wrapped around both of them, pulling them through the door. Then they were flying through a tunnel of swirling light. Without formality, the swirling stopped, and the light plopped them down on a thick cushion of green grass before vanishing behind them.

"Where are we?" Danny asked, eyes as round as golf balls.

Theo jumped to his feet and looked around, mouth gaping at the stunning sight before them.

"I have no idea."

It was more magnificent than anything Theo had seen so far in other earth. He inhaled. The air was sweet, filled with an aroma that consumed him with such wonder that he was afraid to exhale, afraid he would lose the moment.

They stood in a forest surrounded by colossal trees shimmering in hues of blue, yellow, purple, orange, and colors he'd never seen. Their bark seemed to glow, pulsating with the warm light that had pulled them into the book and through the door. It was almost as if the trees themselves were breathing, exhaling the perfumed scent that filled Theo's lungs and mind.

The mystery of Elyon.

"Wow!" Danny breathed, staring at the trees.

Theo lifted his eyes. The sky streamed with brilliant color—golds and reds and greens—and the clouds, like giant pieces of cotton candy floating delicately above them. He could see the sun and the glowing moon, hung side by side. The stars and planets were there too, spinning around one another in a sophisticated dance. It almost seemed to be day and night at the same time, even though that made no sense and went against everything he had learned in school.

Theo leaned down and touched the grass at his feet. It felt like soft velvet. Without thinking, he dropped to his seat, pulled off his Converse and socks, and stood, curling his toes in the carpet of lush grass. It seemed to vibrate with a hint of gentle power that ran through each blade and up through his feet.

"What are you doing?" Danny asked.

"Try it! Take your shoes off! I've never felt anything like it!"

Needing no more encouragement, Danny pulled off his shoes and stood barefoot on the grass. He took a deep breath and sucked in the intoxicating air.

Danny slowly turned his head, soaking in the stunning sights.

A small river flowed beside them with the bright-green waters Theo knew well. This was the same water he'd seen in Elyon's sea. So then . . . Elyon was here somewhere? His heart beat faster and his mind emptied of everything but the boy.

"Hello! Are you here?" he called, hoping for a reply.

There was no sign of the boy anywhere.

Danny looked at him curiously. "Who are you looking for?"

"The boy."

"The boy? You mean Stokes?"

Theo had totally forgotten about Stokes. There was no sign of him either.

"What boy?" Danny asked, looking around. "Do you know where we are?"

Elyon's backyard.

Theo laughed. He didn't know where that thought came from. But he had an idea, a memory of the first time he had seen the boy. With a burst of energy, he ran at Danny and tagged him.

"You're it!" he cried and then took off running.

Danny sprinted behind, laughing as he gave pursuit. The two boys ran through the colored forest with no care for writing assignments, sack lunches outside, or even Asher.

Their pursuit brought them to a bend in the river, and Theo leaned down to sip the water, allowing its gentle power to revive him.

A splash of water hit him in the face. "Hey!" he spluttered, wiping the water away from his eyes enough to see Danny grinning ear to ear. Theo cupped his hand in the water and splashed him back.

"I am here!" a cry came from above, interrupting the water war. They looked up to see Stokes soaring from the sky, carrying their shoes. "Never fear!"

Stokes landed unevenly, tripping on the shoes and tumbling over. He hopped up. "I've brought your clothing!"

"You mean shoes," Theo said, laughing.

"Yes, shoes, of course." Stokes took off and soared high in the enchanted sky. He was like a giant white bird floating above them, maybe showing off a bit or maybe just too overjoyed to remain still.

"Stokes," Theo yelled up to him. "Do you know where we are?"

Stokes landed next to them, grinning ear to ear. "No, but I think we might be in the Realm of the Mystics."

"Where Talya's from?"

"A mystical realm?" Danny walked toward the nearest tree, reached up into the lower branches, and pulled off a giant pink fruit. "Safe?" he asked, eying Stokes.

"I don't see why not."

Danny lifted the fruit to his mouth and took a bite. His eyes closed as he slowly chewed the fruit. Juice dribbled down his chin.

"Wow! You've gotta try this!"

A swarm of fireflies floated down from the trees, one of them landing on Theo's arm. Its little eyes looked up at him. It winked and then lifted into the air, joining its brothers and sisters as they danced in the sky.

Stokes swooped through the fireflies and joined in their performance as they swirled in formation. One by one they lighted on his fluffy body.

"You tickle, little bugs!"

The distant sound of horse hooves pounding against the ground jerked Theo from the fireflies.

Horde? But it couldn't be. Not in this place. He spun toward the sound where the clearing opened into a wide field of grass.

A man on a white horse was riding toward them.

"Who's that?" Danny asked.

"I don't know."

Definitely not Horde.

Stokes landed on the ground beside him, eyes wide.

"Do you know, Stokes?"

"It's . . . it's Justin."

The rider pulled his horse to a stop, looked at them for a moment, then dismounted. He walked toward them. The fireflies moved their attention away from the Roush, swirled around him, and kissed his cheeks with their light.

Justin's eyes were green, like Roush eyes, but something was different about them, something warm and intoxicating, like Elyon's eyes—the boy's eyes.

He had long brown hair that fell to strong shoulders, and he wore leather boots laced up past his ankles. His white tunic was tucked neatly into brown leather pants.

The man stopped a few feet from them and smiled. Then he dipped his head and spread his arms wide.

"Welcome, my dear friends, to the Realm of the Mystics, once called Eden—or as some call it, the Kingdom of Heaven."

The man's voice was deep, smooth, and filled Theo with awe. He knew this man. He knew this man very well.

"You do know me, Theo."

"I do?"

"The last time we met, I was a boy."

"Elyon?"

The man winked. "One and the same. They call me Justin." He lifted his eyes and scanned the horizon. "Do you like what you see?"

"It's beautiful," Danny said. "I can feel it and taste it. I didn't know seeing this way could be so amazing."

"Isn't it? To have the eyes of one who is seeing for the first time is a wonderful thing." Justin looked at Theo. "Learn from Danny. The challenge ahead of you is all about what you see."

Stokes gave a little cough and then stepped forward. One of his ears was flopped over, and his body quivered in amazement.

"It's an honor to see you, Great One," he said, bowing.

"The honor is mine, young Roush. You play an important role in Theo's quests."

Stokes grinned wide. "I do? I mean . . . yes, of course. Thank you!"

"So then . . ." Justin studied Theo and Danny. "Are you ready?"

"Yes," all three said in unison.

Justin nodded once. "Follow me."

The boys stuffed their feet back into their socks and shoes and hurried to catch up with Justin. Theo had no idea what challenge they could possibly have in such a breathtaking place. This third quest was definitely starting out better than the last two.

"This," Justin said, spreading his hands toward the land around them as he walked, "is a picture of reality as it is, beyond the twisted vision that blinds humanity. Remember that; it will come in handy."

Theo had no idea what that could mean, so he followed closely, keeping his questions to himself.

Justin stopped at a wall of vines stretching so far above them that they literally touched the clouds, creating a curtain in front of them. He brushed some of the vines aside, revealing a round, black, wooden door with a large golden hoop for a handle.

"What's this?" Theo asked.

"Your quest," Justin said. "Through this door you will find a world—a temple, if you will. In that temple, you'll encounter three rooms on three different levels. You'll need each other's help if you want to finish. Remember that when you enter. Completing one challenge will reveal the door to the next room."

"Sounds like a video game." Theo considered himself an expert on all things video games. Completing levels and opening doors was the kind of quest he knew well.

"I've always wanted to play a video game," Danny said. "But even if I could've seen them, my foster mom said they'd rot my brain."

Justin chuckled. "You can think of it like a video game—a video game that *won't* rot your brain."

"At the end of the three levels, will we get the third seal?" Theo asked, now fully confident in the easy completion of this quest.

"If you complete all three challenges successfully, you will find the third seal."

"We can do that," Danny said, eying Theo.

Theo bit his lip and nodded. Danny had no idea how difficult things could get in the other world. "Of course we can."

Justin smiled. "Of course you can." He turned to Stokes. "You, my friend, will stay with me for now. The boys must go alone for now."

The last time Theo started a quest without a Roush, he'd found himself locked in a dungeon. Knowing other earth was full of dark surprises, he'd feel much better if Stokes were tagging along.

Justin motioned to the door. "All you have to do is enter."

Theo and Danny exchanged a glance and stepped up to the door. Danny grabbed the handle and pulled. The door creaked open. A rush of cold air poured over them.

Theo peered inside. Pitch black. His heart pounded. He looked back at Justin and Stokes, who both offered encouraging smiles.

"Well, I guess we should go on in."

Theo took a deep breath before walking into the dark with Danny on his heels. The moment they were inside, the door slammed behind them, leaving them in absolute darkness.

"**D**anny?" Theo asked, voice shaking. A hand grabbed his shoulder. He jumped. "Danny, is that you?"

"It's me! I . . . I can't see! I'm blind again!"

"I can't see either. I think it's just the dark."

It's just the dark. It's just the dark. I am the light.

Suddenly, torches burst to life, lining the walls and illuminating a massive room: the first level.

The walls were formed of ancient stone and the ceiling like carefully placed black crystal scales. And the floor underneath was like glass tiles, each etched with the head of a serpent, eerily reflecting the swaying flames.

Two long rows of tall black-granite columns ran down the length of the hall. Piles of treasure—gold, silver, diamonds, and rubies—were heaped all the way to the far end of the room. It reminded Theo of one of the ancient burial sites he'd learned about in history last year. An eerie feeling passed over him, like he was a trespasser in a royal tomb.

Ahead, in the middle of the hall, a massive statue of a bronze snake with piercing red eyes loomed over the room. A large stone coffin rested at the base of the coiled snake.

This was no ordinary room.

"What is this place?" Danny gulped. He walked toward the colossal snake, shoes squeaking on the glass floor.

"I think we're in a tomb," Theo said, following hesitantly behind. It might be like a video game, but it certainly felt real. It was real. "Maybe we shouldn't get too close to that thing."

"Right."

They inched closer. "Look at the columns. There's some kind of writing on them."

"Saying what?" Danny asked.

Along with the strange inscriptions, etchings of snakes coiled between the words. Theo followed the detailed images to the scaled ceiling. He shuddered.

Theo frowned. "It doesn't make sense. It's like in another language or something. Maybe it has something to do with whoever was buried in this tomb."

"You think there's some dead guy in that box?" Danny asked as they approached the sarcophagus.

"I hope not. But it makes sense."

Danny stopped in front of the coffin and reached out his hand.

"Don't touch it!"

"Why not? It's just a big rock." Danny gently brushed his hand across the top. "See? Nothing."

Maybe Danny truly didn't see the harm in messing with an ancient coffin, but Theo had played enough video games to know that scary places usually lead to scary people.

It would be at this point in the game that the background music would shift to something dull and creepy. Theo listened. No music. Another reminder that this was real.

"I think there's something written here," Danny said, rubbing his hand along the side. "Can you read it?"

Danny could only read Braille. Theo leaned forward to see ten words etched into the stone.

"What does it say?"

"'I am the serpent that blinds you again and again,'" Theo read.

He could feel the color drain from his face. He'd heard those words more than once: Shax. Shadow

Man—"And I will blind you over and over again."

"Blinds you?" Danny backed away from the sarcophagus. "I think you're right. We *should* leave it alone."

The lid to the coffin began to tremble and both of them jumped.

"What's happening?" Danny cried, as they hurried backward to put space between them and the coffin.

The stone lid slowly slid to the side and then crashed to the floor, smashing the glass tiles where it hit.

A hand, smooth and perfect, gripped the edge of the stone coffin. Theo watched as a man he knew well slowly rose from inside the coffin and climbed out of the stone grave.

He stood before them in a white shirt and white pants.

Shadow Man.

He smirked, exposing his perfectly white teeth, cracked his neck from left to right, and licked his lips with a long, serpentine tongue. He opened his mouth and let out a bone-chilling hiss that echoed through the hall.

"Welcome to my world."

His body began to twitch and his eyes rolled into the back of his head. In a puff of black smoke, his body morphed into a giant black snake, slowly weaving back and forth, hissing, with his forked tongue flicking at the air.

"Run," Theo whispered. But his feet didn't want to move.

The snake hissed again, edging closer.

"Run!" Danny screamed. He spun, ran straight into Theo, and then pushed past him. Theo raced after him, close on his heels, back the way they'd come.

But the black circular door they'd entered through was gone.

"Where's the door? We have to find a way out!" Danny cried.

The sound of the slithering serpent's hissing was closing from behind.

Theo looked from side to side. If they stayed where they were, they'd be snake food in a matter of minutes.

"This way!" Theo shouted, taking off for the right side of the room. He slid to his knees behind a large mound of gold coins, breathing hard.

This is a game. Just a game. If I die . . .

If he died, did he get another life? Did he have multiple lives? Could he earn extra lives?

Danny dropped in beside him. "Where's the snake? Maybe if we can't see it, it can't see us."

"I doubt it works that way."

"Then we have to get out!"

"We can't get out! There's a snake out there!"

He looked behind him, searching for any sign of the snake, which was momentarily leaving them alone. But he knew this kind of snake. It had a plan, and it wouldn't leave them alone until it got what it wanted.

Danny peered around the edge. "Where did it go?"

Theo held his breath and listened as best he could. The hissing had ceased. He crept forward and looked around the pile with Danny. Nothing.

"You think it's gone?" Danny whispered.

"I doubt it." Theo knew Shadow Man's game. He would wait until the perfect moment and then strike with his twisted words.

Danny slowly stretched his body up straight and inched out from behind the pile of treasure. "It's gone."

"Get back here!"

But Danny was being brave again. "It's gone! Maybe we did it."

"We didn't do anything. There was no battle, no riddle to solve." Theo stood up, craning for a view of a tail, a scale, anything that might be snake. Nothing.

But there was no chance they'd escaped. It was never that easy.

"Ah! What was that?" Danny jumped, wiping a glob of gooey clear fluid off his shoulder. A slow hiss resonated around the room.

The boys hesitantly glanced up and saw it. Directly above them the snake had coiled itself around a massive iron chandelier, watching patiently. Waiting for them.

"Run!" Theo shouted. "Run, Danny!"

But Danny didn't run. He stood motionless, trembling from head to foot. The huge serpent dropped down, wrapped itself around Danny, and pulled him to the floor, binding him in its scaly skin.

Theo raced toward his friend, ignoring the voice in his head that said there was nothing he could do.

Before he could close the distance, the snake opened its jaw wide and hissed out a black smoke that swirled around Danny. The fog seeped into his ears and covered his eyes.

"I can't see! Theo! Help me!"

Fear for his friend's life consumed Theo. He ran full force into the snake's side and began pounding his fists into its scaled body.

He continued to beat, one hand after another, until he realized there was no longer anything to hit.

He opened his eyes to find himself in a brightly lit clearing. Danny was on the ground screaming, eyes clenched tight. Theo stood frozen for a moment, trying to grasp where they were. Had they succeeded?

Theo spun around. Justin leaned against a tree, arms crossed, smiling. They were back outside the black door.

He leaned down and shook his new friend.

"Danny, it's okay. We aren't there anymore."

Danny stopped screaming and opened his eyes. "I can see. I can see!" Stokes grabbed Danny's hand to pull him up.

Theo turned to Justin. "What happened?"

"You let fear control you. Fear always distorts your vision. Know that you must find a way past your distorted vision."

Danny stared at him, unsure. "Try again?"

"Try again," Justin said. "You have to complete the challenge without losing sight."

"But how?" Danny demanded. "It's a huge snake and there's nothing we can do! There's nowhere to hide. And it had this stuff that comes out of its mouth. It . . . it blinded me. "

Justin arched his brow. "Really? Or maybe you were blind the moment you stepped inside the room."

"No, I could see."

"See what? The room? Maybe there's more to see."

Theo thought about that. It actually made sense. They hadn't been blind to the room, but Justin was saying that they were blind to something else. What? What was he not seeing?

"We need help. Is there something we're missing?"

"I can give you one more hint. Find the glasses

that will help you see what's to be seen."

Talya had said that they would no longer be blind if they found the right lenses. Glasses.

Justin winked. "Think of them as corrective lenses. In this game, everyone needs them. Without them, he will blind you again and again."

Not this time, Theo thought.

The door slammed behind them for the second time. Anxiety welled up inside of Theo. He thought it would be easier the second time, knowing what was about to happen. But the expectation made the room even more frightening.

"If this is like a video game, then everything that happened the first time should happen again."

First, the flames.

The flames burst into life exactly as they had done before, illuminating the room, its piles of treasure, and the huge serpent statue in their eerie flickering light.

"Right," Danny said, taking a deep breath. "It's just a game. I have to remember that. Just like a video game . . . with a huge snake."

"Let's think," Theo said. "The torches lit. The

sarcophagus opened. Shadow Man turned into the snake—"

"Shadow Man?"

"I'll explain when we get out of here."

"He's going to blind me again. I just know it!" Danny's confidence was gone.

"We have to find the glasses before that happens." Theo scanned the room. He had to think like a gamer. There was only one place to look. "We have to search the treasure."

"That will take forever."

"Unless you want to go diggin' around Shadow Man's tomb, it's our only option. You search to the right. I'll go left. Open every box! Look for glasses."

He began his search, tossing aside gold-plated shields and handfuls of coins. He wiped sweat away from his forehead with the back of his arm. Danny was right; this *could* take forever. And they didn't have forever. A moment of defeat passed over him. How could he find something so small in such huge mounds of treasure? They could be anywhere!

Still, he had to try.

Any other time he would definitely be focused on how many coins he could stuff in the pockets of his blue jeans. But they were about to be chased and pummeled by a gargantuan snake. The treasure might as well be a pile of trash.

"Found anything?" Danny called out from the other side.

"Not yet!" Theo hurried around the golden mound, scanning for anything that looked like glasses. He scrambled up and pushed back a golden suit of armor, exposing a golden chest. He tossed open the lid. Empty. He found another one. Empty. Then another. Empty.

All empty. Time was running out.

"Anything?" Danny called again, voice tight. His brave new friend was afraid. Theo couldn't blame him, but it didn't help to settle his own nerves.

"Keep looking!" Theo called.

He gave up on the first pile and ran to the next one, casting a quick glance at the stone sarcophagus under the serpent statue. Closed. Maybe it only opened if touched the way Danny had the first time. That would give them all the time they needed. He could only hope.

The next heap offered nothing more than the first.

A loud scraping sound suddenly filled the room. Theo jerked his eyes toward the coffin.

"It's happening again!" Danny cried out from across the room.

The stone lid trembled, slowly sliding open. They were running out of time!

"Keep looking!" Theo yelled, racing for another pile as panic prickled at the back of his neck. The search was beginning to feel hopeless.

A crash echoed through the room. The lid was off! Theo spun to see Shadow Man slowly rise from the sarcophagus and step out. He turned his head, looked at Theo, and offered a wicked grin.

Theo froze, lost in hopelessness. He would gladly trade all the treasure in the room for those glasses, but now it was too late.

Another hiss shook the room. It was happening again.

"I think I found them!" Danny shouted. "Hurry!"

Moving as fast as his legs would carry him, Theo raced toward Danny's voice. Crossing the room, he watched as the snake rose from the smoke and flicked its tongue out, tacking him with evil eyes. It was coming.

Theo scrambled up one of the piles and tumbled down the other side. He found Danny kneeling beside a simple, rectangular wooden box. In his hands he held a pair of old glasses with gold rims. Theo dropped to his knees beside Danny and looked in the box. There was a second pair.

Hissing echoed around them. The snake was slithering closer.

"Put them on!" Theo said, grabbing the second pair.

He pushed the glasses onto his nose and watched as the world around him transformed.

He could see through the piles of treasure! Almost as if they, along with everything else in the room, were a dimly glowing holographic image or a bizarre shifting energy.

Incredible!

"Do you see it?" Danny asked.

The huge snake was approaching fast, hissing as it slithered straight for them. "Of course I see the snake!"

"No, the giant glowing circle," Danny said, pointing to the back of the room.

A large circle glowed bright on the back wall, like a button beckoning them to push it.

"It wasn't there before!" Danny said.

"That has to be our way out." Theo looked back in the direction of the snake. "Where'd it go? Where's the snake?"

"There . . ." Danny pointed up at the gothic chandelier between them and the circle.

Theo looked at the circle and then up at the snake. It was watching them, patiently studying them. Waiting for them to make their next move. This was not good.

"If it drops before we get to the other side, we'll never make it," Danny whispered.

"We'll have to run for it."

"But it's faster than us!"

Danny was right. Theo had another idea. "We distract it, divert its attention. Then we stick to the columns. It can't chase what it can't see. But you have to run this time. Okay?"

"Okay."

"I'll distract it, then you go!" Theo slowly reached down, keeping his eyes locked on the snake. He grasped a gold goblet and carefully straightened. "Get ready." With all his might he flung the goblet to the other side of the room.

"Run!"

The goblet clanged to the ground. The creature flinched and hissed. The boys tore toward the nearest column. They reached it, panting, backs pressed against the black granite. The minor distraction had worked.

"Go!"

They took off running again, their feet pounding against the glass floor.

A loud thump echoed through the room. The snake had dropped. Heart slamming in his chest, Theo abandoned the notion that the columns would keep them hidden.

"We have to go straight for the circle!"

Theo abandoned the columns and ran with Danny at his side. He didn't look back, eyes on the glowing circle. If they could only make it . . .

A hissing to his right pushed him faster than he'd ever run, arms pumping, legs thrashing forward.

He cried out as something wrapped itself around his leg, plucked him from the ground and jerked him into the air, feet above his head.

He twisted and shook, screaming, trying desperately to get free of the strong coils wrapped around his ankles.

But it was no use. He dangled in the air, watching as the snake twisted its head and came in for the kill.

Theo screamed.

"Theo!" Danny was screaming for him.

The snake's tongue flickered in the air, hissing, watching Theo with evil eyes. Blood filled Theo's head as he dangled in its grasp, helpless.

"Theo," the snake hissed, "didn't I promise to blind you again and again? I will win one way or another, boy." Its tongue tasted the air again. "Even if it means finding you in your world, I will blind you."

Shadow Man could cross over?

But he had bigger problems right now.

The snake brought its mouth close to Theo's face and breathed. Black smoke flooded his face. *This is it! He's going to blind me! I'll never see again.*

The black vapor swirled around him, flowed up to his face, then backed away. The vapor tried again, hovering in front of his eyes and then falling to his feet. It only took Theo a moment to realize what had happened. The glasses! They were protecting his eyes!

The snake pulled back and hissed furiously. Then it turned Theo upright and slammed him into one of the columns. Pain flashed through him as his body collided with stone. The snake blew its smoke out again, but once again, it didn't affect Theo.

Below him, Danny was shouting furiously. From the corner of his eye, Theo caught sight of him running toward the snake with a golden sword. He plunged the blade into the side of the snake. Thrashing, its grip on Theo relaxed and Theo suddenly found himself falling. He landed on the floor with a painful thump.

"Hurry!" Danny cried, tugging at his arm. "Run!"

Theo rose, wobbly on his feet, and staggered forward as Danny took off. Then Theo was giving chase, fleeing the snake and sprinting toward the back wall.

The gold circle glowed brightly in front of them. Doing his best to ignore the hissing snake behind them, Theo slammed both hands into the middle of the circle.

A ball of light shot out from the circle. Theo gasped as the circle began to recede into the wall. The room shook violently, knocking both Theo and Danny from their feet.

"The room's collapsing!" Danny cried, hugging the quaking floor. The snake was gone, replaced by the sound of a furious scream.

Spinning around, Theo saw the ball of light that had come from the circle hovering over the huge serpent statue in the middle of the room.

The ball of light hung there for a few seconds and then suddenly detonated like a starburst, flooding the room. Theo twisted back and covered his head as warm light washed over his back. He lay still, face down, afraid to look up.

The room went silent.

"Theo?"

Theo slowly raised his head to see Danny looking over him. They were no longer in the dark tomb. He gasped.

They were in what looked like a royal ballroom. They were still in the same room, but it had been transformed into a beautiful white room with gold trim and a magnificent crystal chandelier glowing in the center. The mounds of gold were replaced by large chests, probably each holding treasure. The columns still stood but were made of crystal.

No snake. No Shadow Man.

"Wow," Danny said, pushing himself up from the floor. The glasses on Danny's face suddenly turned to sand and fell away.

Theo reached up and touched his face. His glasses were gone too.

"We beat the first level," Theo whispered.

The wall next to them began to move. Where

the circle had once glowed, an opening appeared, revealing a set of stone stairs.

The next level. Another challenge. He wasn't sure he was ready. His body ached from its impact with the column, and a drink of water sure would be nice.

"The second level!" Danny said, looking up the stairs. He stepped eagerly forward.

"Hold on," Theo said, grabbing his shoulder. "You sure we shouldn't rest up a bit?"

"Here?" Danny looked back at the ballroom and then up the stairs. "Don't you want to see what's up there?"

Now that he thought about it, he did. In fact, there was no guarantee the opening in the wall would remain open.

Theo nodded. "Let's go."

The boys climbed up the stone stairs and found themselves at another door. Theo grabbed the handle, took a deep breath, and pulled.

As it creaked open, the stairs behind them began to crumble.

"Jump!" Theo threw himself through the doorway, landing on a damp concrete floor. There was no going back.

The door clanged shut, leaving them out of breath and once again in the dark.

D*ark again*, Theo thought, attempting to scramble to his feet. Pain pulsated through his body.

He had just been tossed around by an evil snake and had escaped a disintegrating room. For all of that, he would have thought he'd get some kind of reward—a power-up, credits, extra lives, something—not another room in darkness. This wouldn't be a very popular game back home.

Then again, the third seal was the ultimate reward. They'd only beaten one level. Justin's words returned to him: "Find a way to see past everything that might distort your vision."

Apparently, this whole game was about finding a way to see in a new way, like seeing in the darkness. And special glasses could do that. It was like getting new eyes.

Danny touched Theo's arm. "You okay? That slam against the column looked like it hurt. "

"I'll live," Theo said with a fake chuckle. "I'm just glad we made it to the second level."

"Which means we won't have to repeat the first level, even if we fail, right?"

"That's how it is in every game I've played. I mean, unless you want to go back and play it again."

"No, thanks!"

Theo tried to focus in the dark. His pulse increased. This was no ordinary darkness. He could almost feel it sinking into his skin, searching for a host, like a living organism.

Remember who you are.

The darkness fought against the truths of the first two seals. He tried to think about what he knew to be true, but he feared the darkness might swallow him up if he wasn't careful.

Think, Theo.

"Last time the light just came on, but I have a feeling that's not how this room works or we'd have light by now."

"Let me see if I can find anything," Danny said.

Theo grabbed his arm. "Wait, what are you doing? Don't leave me."

He didn't like being left alone in the dark. Why

couldn't he get past this? He had the first two seals, right?

"All right, hold onto my shirt," Danny said, moving effortlessly forward. "This is kind of funny, don't you think?"

"Funny? Are you seeing something I don't? What if we trip over something? Aren't you the least bit afraid?"

He felt like Annelee with all her questions.

"For one, I'm not afraid of the dark. Never have been. It's all I've ever known. It's my normal. And my other senses are sharp, so I can feel surfaces and even temperature changes pretty well. It's funny because I'm leading you! I've never led anyone before. Come on."

"Well, I'm not afraid either. I'm just . . ." As they stepped forward, Theo could feel something wet seeping into the canvas of his Converse. "Do you feel that? We're walking through water or something."

"I know. It has a smell too."

Theo sniffed the warm air. "I don't smell anything."

"There is a slight buzzing sound over this way. It's like the sound of a light switch."

"You can hear a light switch?"

"Sometimes."

Theo tried to listen, but again, nothing. "I don't hear it."

"Just keep walking," Danny said, leading the way. A few minutes later, he took Theo's hand and placed it on something smooth and cold. "I think it's a wall. Wait here."

Theo waited, hearing Danny slosh through the water. Then he heard the click of a switch. The room flooded with a bright florescent light. Danny stood smiling, standing on a diamond-shaped slab of concrete with this hand on a black rope that hung from the ceiling above him.

The space was large, octagonal in shape, and mirrored from floor to ceiling. The rusty-red water-filled floor appeared to slope downward toward the hard platform on which Danny stood. There was no way out that he could see.

Danny hopped off his perch with a splash, spraying Theo with the water. He sloshed over to the mirror and studied his reflection. He watched himself feel his hair and study his clothing. He opened his mouth and stuck out his tongue. "It's me. Mirrors."

He stopped his examination and scanned the room. "There's nothing to be afraid of here. It's just us."

Theo sloshed through the tinted water to the concrete platform. He scanned the room—same on all eight sides: only mirrors, the black rope hanging from the center of the ceiling, and nothing else.

He studied the mirrors. He saw himself and Danny, but there was also a faint outline of someone . . . something else. He looked closer.

"I don't think so. Do you see that?" he asked, pulse pounding.

Danny squinted as he examined the mirror. Suddenly, something slammed its hand up against the glass from inside. He jumped back. "Ahh! What is that?"

Theo spun around only to find some kind of creature staring at him from another mirror. It had horns and its head was cocked as it looked at him.

Theo grabbed Danny, pulled him up on the platform, and pointed. But Danny was looking at another mirror, arm extended and trembling. He followed Danny's finger to a man standing behind the mirror—a man with no eyes.

Every mirror encaged a monster, trapped behind what appeared to be nothing more than a thin piece of glass.

"What is this?" Danny asked, voice quivering.

"My greatest nightmares come to life."

"But it's part of the game. We can beat it, right?"

It didn't feel like a game anymore. "We need the glasses."

"Where do we look?"

There were no doors to other rooms, no boxes, no cabinets—nothing but the concrete platform they were on, the mirrors, and the water.

"In the water. The glasses have to be in the water!" Frantic, Theo jumped off the platform and into the water, refusing to look up at the mirrors.

Danny followed, jumping back into the murk.

As if sensing Theo's fear, the monsters began to tap and then pound on the mirrors from the other side.

"Hurry!" He trudged through the rusty knee-deep water. He needed to get closer, go deeper. He

knelt down. The water covered his arms up to his biceps, soaking his blue jeans and his T-shirt. But he didn't care. They had to find the glasses!

Assuming there were glasses to be found.

The pounding increased, shaking the walls and rippling the water.

His fingers bumped into something solid. Something square. He grabbed the object and lifted it from the water.

Wooden. The size of a shoebox.

"I think I found it!"

Theo tromped back to the safety of the hard platform and scrambled up as Danny rolled onto it, dripping wet. On his knees, he pulled open the box lid. Two pairs of glasses lay inside. They were like the ones they'd used on the first level, but this time black instead of gold-rimmed.

He quickly pulled out a pair and placed them on his face. Danny snatched up the other pair.

His heart soared as the frames settled on his nose, knowing that they would soon be done with this level. He looked up and stared around the room, waiting for a door to appear or a circle to glow like on the first level.

But nothing changed. Nothing at all.

And then, something did change—Danny. Theo's

courageous friend was gawking at one of the mirrors, backing away in terror.

"What is it?" Theo demanded, looking at the mirror where Danny was staring.

"You . . . you don't see them?" Danny cried.

"See what?"

"The snakes! They're coming out of the mirror!"

Danny flung himself off the platform and back into the water.

"Get ahold of yourself, Danny! There's nothing there."

Danny was suddenly jerked down, deeper into the water. He began to scream, flailing in panic.

"Get them off! Get them off me! Make them stop!"

Theo felt his gut turn as Danny's fear spread to him. He looked around frantically.

"I don't see anything!" He leaped into the water to help Danny. "There's nothing on you! What do you want me to do?"

Danny seemed to have lost his mind.

"Stop it!" Theo yelled, frightened by Danny's panic. "There's nothing here!"

"Get them off! Get them—"

Without finishing his sentence, Danny stopped flailing his arms. His body stiffened, his lips trembled, and his eyes widened. Theo watched in stunned horror as a black fog came up from the water and swirled around the glass frames on his face. Danny's eyes turned black.

No! That's not possible! He's wearing the glasses!

"Danny?" Theo shook him, but Danny didn't move.

A loud thump sounded behind Theo. He jerked around and watched with stunned disbelief as a creature slowly crawled through the mirror and into the room.

His lungs tightened. He couldn't breathe.

It wasn't just any monster. This one looked like Asher but with black bat ears, sharp fangs, and long claws. It was a cross between Shataiki and the bully from school.

The monster's eyes fixed on him as it plodded forward through the water. Theo felt his face drain of blood. His insides screamed, terrified. He willed his body to move, to run, to find safety, but it refused to obey him. He stood like a statue, frozen by terror.

The creature's eyes narrowed and its lips parted into a wicked smile as it stepped onto the platform. It reached out with its claws, grabbed his shirt and jerked him forward so that Theo's face was inches from the beast's fanged mouth.

A black fog that smelled like rotting eggs washed over him, around the glasses on his face, and into his eyes.

The world around him went black.

The creature released him. Theo crumpled to the floor as the creature receded, chuckling under its raspy breath.

Theo lay in complete darkness. His eyes were open, but he could see nothing. Both he and Danny were blind. Fear smothered him.

"Help!" he screamed.

But somewhere in that scream he became aware that the surface under him was no longer the hard platform. He was on grass.

Light flooded his eyes and the world came back into view.

They were back in the garden.

Theo sat up with Danny next to him, eyes red and teary. Danny breathed out and swallowed hard, taking a few seconds to collect himself. He turned his head away, wiping at his eyes. Theo assumed Danny didn't want anyone to see him cry.

Justin stood to his left, watching them with kind eyes. Stokes stared awkwardly, as if he wanted to help but was unsure how he could.

"Danny," Justin said in a gentle voice, "tell Theo what you saw."

Danny looked up at Justin and then looked at Theo. "I saw my greatest fear. It was everywhere. All around me. And then it blinded me."

Theo had seen his greatest fear too. He looked up at Justin. "My fear was a monster that looked like Asher, but it was also Shataiki. It blinded me too."

Theo paused and turned to Danny. "You kept saying that snakes were coming for you. Are snakes your greatest fear?"

Danny shook his head. "No. Not really. It's what they were saying."

"What were they saying?"

Danny stared at the grass, silent.

Justin stepped over and crouched down. "They told Danny that he would never be wanted, that he would always be alone."

Danny lifted his eyes to Justin. Tears slipped from his dark brown eyes. This time, he didn't hide them.

"I've always been alone," he said. "My parents died when I was really young, and since then I've bounced around the system. No one wants a blind kid. I'm too much work. It won't be long before I'm moved again."

Theo had a dad who loved him. He couldn't imagine how Danny felt living a life not knowing that love.

"You both let your fears blind you," Justin said. "You allowed them to consume you, and once you are consumed, you can't see the truth. It's nothing to be ashamed of—most people live in fear most of their lives, hardly knowing how deep they run. Either way, fear always blinds you."

"But we did the second level right," Theo said. "We put on the glasses. Nothing happened."

Justin rose. "Nothing? But you're wrong. They did plenty."

"Our fears came through the mirrors when we put the glasses on," Danny said. "Was that supposed to happen?"

"Sometimes we allow ourselves to look through the wrong lenses. When you look through the lenses of the world, you see fear instead of love, darkness instead of light. It's blindness of a whole different kind. It's a blindness in which you think you can see, but what you're seeing is a lie."

"So we put on the wrong glasses?" Theo asked.

"You need the glasses of the Kingdom."

"Isn't that what we put on? They were the same as the glasses we found in the first—"

"No," Danny interrupted, jumping to his feet. "They weren't. The ones we put on in the first level had gold around the edges. The ones we put on in the second room were black."

Theo shot up. "You're right."

"So maybe if we find the gold-edged glasses, we will be able to see past our fears and move to the next room."

Theo looked at Justin for confirmation.

Justin winked, filling him with encouragement. "Want to try again?"

"Yes." Danny grabbed Theo by the shirt and pulled him toward the door.

He was just about the bravest kid Theo had ever met.

"Remember," Justin said, "no one can see past their fears without changing their perception. For that you need the right lenses."

"Of course," Danny said, as if it were now the most obvious thing in the world. He looked at Theo. "Ready?"

"Ready."

They pulled together and the door swung open, revealing the dark room. Theo latched onto Danny's shirt. The door slammed shut behind them, leaving them in complete darkness once more.

"I'm right behind you."

Danny trudged toward the center of the dark room with Theo linked behind him. The cold water once again soaked his clothing. They climbed up on the platform. Then the flood of light filled the mirrored space as Danny pulled the black rope.

The memory of the fear he'd felt the last time engulfed his mind. *What if we can't find—*

His thought was cut short by a slam behind him.

The hand! It was back, slapping the other side of the mirror.

The man with no eyes was pressed against the mirror, banging his hands on the glass, trying to get out. One by one the monsters materialized, clawing against the mirrors that encaged them.

"I hate this room," Theo breathed, trying to slow his racing pulse.

"We have to find the other glasses," Danny breathed, eyes fixed on the mirrors.

Theo jumped back in the water, searching frantically. But he couldn't focus. He stood, attempting to drown out the sounds of the monsters' cries. It was too much. He stooped down again, hands sifting through the who-knows-what in the water. The memory of Shadow Man's voice stopped his search: "I will win one way or another, boy. Even if it means finding you in your world, I will blind you."

Even if he found the glasses this time, would Shadow Man find him—at home, in school, with his dad? It couldn't be true. He had to focus on what he knew to be true. He had to find the glasses!

But why was he so afraid? He knew what he had to do. And if they failed, Justin and Stokes were waiting for them.

As Theo slogged through the water, the answer came to him. He was afraid of his own fear, afraid he would feel fear again, which he was. He knew the game was all an illusion—part of his quest to find the third seal—but he was afraid of the fear the illusion would make him feel.

It was a staggering thought. How much of life was like that?

The monsters kept banging, desperate to escape the confines of their cages.

Danny and Theo rushed through the water, hands searching the murkiness at their feet.

"Hurry!" Danny cried.

Theo took a deep breath and tried to calm himself, attempting to stop the fear from washing through him. Fear was just a feeling.

It can't hurt me. Focus. Find the glasses.

He took another deep breath and coughed. *Ugh.* Danny was right. There was a smell—sour and metallic. He methodically covered the bottom of the shallow pool using both hands. They needed to find a different box this time.

His fingers grazed something hard in the water. He pulled the object out. The wooden box he had found before rested in his hands. He opened it to see the black-rimmed glasses.

"Did you find it?" Danny called, jerking upright.

"Wrong ones," he said, slamming the lid closed. The thought of looking through the lenses of the world terrified him. Not this time. Not a chance!

He impulsively flung the box at the wall and winced when it hit the mirror. What if the mirror broke and released the monster?

But the box banged harmlessly on the glass and splashed to the ground.

"I think I found it!" Danny cried from the other side of the room.

Theo spun around. "You sure?"

Danny opened the box, looked inside, beaming. "Think so."

Theo sloshed over to him, eager. He peered into the box. Two pairs of gold glasses rested inside. His heart jumped.

"That's them!" He grabbed one pair and shoved the glasses over his nose.

As with the first level, the room took on a golden glow. He looked around, trying to find an exit. Nothing.

Nothing except the monsters. But he wasn't afraid anymore. It was as if the glasses stripped him of the power fear had on him.

The sudden release of that fear was so powerful that his whole body felt like it was floating.

Danny looked at him from behind his own glasses, eyes wide.

"Wow!" he said, swallowing deeply. "I feel . . ."

There were no words to describe the release from fear.

"I know," he said, scanning the room. "Do you see a way out?"

"No," Danny said, turning in circles. "Do you see the monsters?"

"They're there, but they look different."

Danny walked up to the closest mirror and stared inside.

"What are you doing?"

But then Theo saw them: snakes, slithering on top of each other as they thumped their bodies against the glass.

Danny slowly lifted his hand and placed it against the glass. Theo knew exactly what he was doing. He was facing what once frightened him without fear—with new sight.

Danny closed his eyes and took a deep breath. "You don't scare me anymore."

The glass in front of Danny began to vibrate, cracking the mirror from top to bottom. The snakes inside hissed and scurried back.

Theo stepped up to the mirror next to Danny

and placed his palms on the cold glass. The monster he had created from his fear moved forward. Asher snarled as blood dripped from his fangs. But this time, Theo felt no fear.

He closed his eyes. "You don't scare me."

The sounds of cracking mirrors filled the room. The Asher monster in front of him began to shrink back.

Filled with courage, Theo pushed harder and said the first thing that came to mind. "Leave."

With those words, the glass walls burst into thousands of tiny shards. They floated, suspended in the air for a few seconds, and then fell into the water.

As soon as the shattered pieces of mirror splashed into the water, the room changed. The water vanished and the monsters disappeared.

The boys were left surrounded by eight white walls with golden trim. In one of those walls, moments earlier hidden by the mirrors, rested a small door.

A way out.

"We did it! We beat the second level!" Theo's glasses turned to sand and vanished before the grains could hit the floor.

"Now what?" Danny asked, looking at the door, his glasses gone.

"The next level."

But he wasn't sure he was ready for the next level.

The third seal of truth.

He began to pace. "We have to remember what this is all about."

"What do you mean, remember? It's about surviving this game."

"But it's not really a game. We're here to find the third seal of truth. I've been so caught up in beating these monsters that I keep forgetting all about our real quest."

He pulled up his shirtsleeve and stared at the two circles on his shoulder. The first seal was white. *Elyon is the light.* The second seal was green. *I am the light of the world.* But if that was true, why was he always finding himself in darkness?

"Your dad let you get a tattoo?"

Theo laughed. "No. I got them when I found the seals. It helps me remember . . . until I forget they're there, which seems to happen more than it should."

"Did it hurt?"

"No." Theo turned to the door.

"So this third truth," Danny said, "what do you think it is?"

"I think it has something to with sight and seeing beyond our fears. Turning our blindness into sight. Maybe. I don't know."

"Makes sense."

Theo sighed. "We just keep seeing things wrong. I keep forgetting what I should know."

"So, when we get to the next level we find the Kingdom glasses right away. We don't give ourselves time to forget!"

"Maybe." He wasn't so sure. "But it can't be that simple. In video games the levels get harder."

They stared at the door for a few seconds.

"Okay," Theo said and let out a long breath. "Let's go."

Danny followed Theo to the door, which opened with a twist of a knob.

"Ready?"

Danny gave him a nod.

Theo pushed the door open. A narrow stone passageway lay ahead, lit by two torches. Seemed plain enough.

"Let's go."

The moment they stepped into the tunnel, the door slammed shut behind them.

Level three.

"What do you think's down there?" Danny asked.

"We're going to find out."

A slow hiss resonated down the tunnel.

"Snakes?" Danny whispered.

"No, I don't think so. Sounds different."

"Then what?"

Theo hesitated, unnerved. "Shataiki."

"Shataiki?"

"They're—"

"I know. You told me . . . evil."

The door behind them suddenly burst open. The boys spun around. There, framed by a warm glow, stood Stokes, blinking at them.

"Stokes!" Theo said. "What are you doing here? You nearly gave me a heart attack."

Stokes waddled through the doorway and grinned sheepishly. "Justin sent me. He said you might need my help now."

"Help with what?"

Stokes only shrugged, grinning widely.

That wasn't very encouraging.

The Roush pulled two staffs from behind him, similar to the one Elyon had given Theo—the one Shadow Man had broken.

Stokes handed one to each of them. "In case we run into Shataiki."

Another hiss echoed in the hallway, and Theo gripped his staff.

With a cry, Stokes leaped around them and landed in a fighting stance, fully alert.

"Never fear! Follow me."

The sound of hissing increased as Stokes lead the way, on guard and in charge, but he appeared to be as nervous as Theo. At any moment one of those beasts could come flying out of the darkness.

"You've encountered these Shataiki before, right?" Danny asked, keeping close behind.

"Yes," Theo whispered.

A moment passed before Danny pressed for more.

"And what happened?"

"A battle."

Silence. Then finally he asked the pressing question. "You won?"

"I'm alive, aren't I?" Theo said. He'd fill in the details later. Now was not the time to tell Danny that he had actually failed miserably upon their first encounter.

Stokes shot up his hand. "Stop."

Theo gazed past him and saw what Stokes saw: a pair of red eyes glowing in the dark, then two pair, and then ten pair. Theo held his breath. He'd fought the beasts before, but he could only think of that first encounter—tied up, with Shax breathing into his face. What were they thinking heading right toward the bats?

The Shataiki came suddenly, shrieking death cries that sent shivers down his spine.

He forgot how to breathe. Their fangs could easily tear out his throat.

Danny screamed.

Stokes leaped into the air, spinning, leg chambered for a roundhouse kick. His foot slammed into the lead Shataiki's jaw, sending it reeling back into several others. The tangled mob fell to the ground.

Theo clenched his eyes tightly and then opened them. *Elyon is the light. I am the son of Elyon. Nothing can threaten him. I am the light of the world.*

"Come on!" he cried, tearing at the fallen Shataiki scrambling for footing. "Now, while they're down!" He swung his staff blindly into the black furred mob and was rewarded by shrieks and wails.

Claws grabbed at his shoulder as one of them latched onto him from behind. But before Theo could react, a deadly thump sounded and the claws released him.

He spun around to see Danny, staff in hand, staring at the fallen Shataiki at his feet. He looked up, eyes bright. And then Danny was flying forward, fully engaged, screaming like a howler monkey as he tore into the onrushing Shataiki.

Clearly, Danny was a natural-born fighter. Being blind, this was probably the first time he'd done anything remotely similar.

Both Danny and Stokes tore into the Shataiki, leaving those who got past them to Theo—like the one that was rushing straight for him, flashing red eyes locked on him.

Theo planted his feet as the beast flew in, waiting for the exact moment to act. He swung his staff like a baseball bat. It cracked against the Shataiki's head and sent it careening into the far wall.

The bat plummeted to the ground in a heap of black fur.

"Keep moving!" Stokes yelled as he took down another beast.

They hardly needed any encouragement. Their feet pounded against the dirt as they ran. The Shataiki continued their advance from behind, but they were hesitant, as if their confidence had been shaken. However, all it would take was one fang in the neck and things would go very wrong.

The end of the tunnel loomed. A round hatch sealed it off.

Stokes dropped to the ground. "Get through the hatch and I'll hold them off!"

Theo slammed into the metal hatch, shoved the handle down and pushed hard. It fell in and clattered noisily on the ground.

"Hurry!" He shoved Danny through and then dove through behind him.

Stokes flew past them. "Seal it. They're coming!"

They lifted the hatch and slammed it back into place just as the first Shataiki reached it. There was a loud thump, followed by a yelp, as the black beast crashed into the other side of the metal door.

They stepped back, breathing hard.

"Yikes," Danny said.

Theo turned around and scanned the huge room. He recognized it immediately as a library. But it was much bigger than the one at school.

They stood on a long, narrow red rug that was rolled out in front of them and ran the length of the diamond-shaped room. At least ten rows of bookshelves made of some kind of ancient wood lined both sides. At the center hung a beautiful, glittering golden chandelier like the one in the ballroom. Theo considered checking it for snakes.

"Wow, this is cool," Danny said, stepping onto the red rug.

"I have a bad feeling about this place," Stokes said.

A chill snaked down Theo's neck. Something about this room didn't feel right. It was beautiful and seemed harmless enough, but he felt as if something rotten was growing beneath the surface.

As if in response to Theo's thought, the rug under him moved.

All three of them leaped off to the side, startled.

But it wasn't just the rug. The whole room seemed to be coming alive. The walls wavered in and out, pulsating, breathing. The books looked less like books and more like . . .

Scales.

A hiss echoed around them.

As fast as the room had distorted, it reverted back into its original shape, leaving them in a quiet library once again.

For a long moment, all three of them stared at the walls, wide-eyed, expecting them to move again. But they were just library walls.

Theo had no doubt things were about to get a whole lot worse.

He spun around, scanning the room. "We've got to find the glasses. We need to find them now!"

Danny ran toward the closest bookshelf. "Look for boxes on the shelves."

"Split up to cover more ground," Theo said, spinning to Stokes. "Go with Danny to that side, and I'll take this side."

"Are you sure?"

"Better yet, fly up and search the tops of the shelves."

"Got it!" Stokes said, leaping into the air.

"If anything goes wrong, meet at the center under the chandelier."

Theo ran between two rows and scanned the shelves for any kind of box that might hold the glasses. To his surprise, he spotted a box almost immediately—fourth shelf. He climbed up, grabbed the box nestled between two books, and hoped he'd found the right one.

He tucked the box under his arm and climbed back down. Then he pulled the lid open.

Glasses!

Glasses with brown rims, not the golden rims of the Kingdom glasses. His heart sank. There was no telling what putting these glasses on would make him see. He wasn't about to find out.

Theo dropped the box and kept looking. He found four more boxes tucked away into the bookshelves, but each one had the wrong kind of frame—blue, purple, black, pink, but no gold.

"Any luck?" he called out, hoping Danny or Stokes were faring better.

"They're all the wrong ones!" Danny's voiced echoed back.

The room shook. Theo cringed.

Before his eyes, the books morphed back into shiny, black scales. They really were inside of a snake!

Theo turned and sprinted toward the center of the library. The moment his foot landed on the red carpet, he confirmed their suspicions. The soft rug squished under his tennis shoes. He jumped off and watched as it lifted up and down, like a long tongue slowly coming to life.

"Did that just happen?" Danny asked, peering around from behind one of the bookshelves.

Theo scratched his head. Scales were on the outside of a snake and the tongue on the inside. They couldn't be on both the outside and the inside. Unless . . .

"Is it just me, or do you get the feeling this room is morphing into a snake?"

"A snake?"

It made sense. Shadow Man had taken the form of a snake on the first level. Fear had taken the form of snakes on the second level.

Now on the third level, they were actually witnessing the transformation. And in a matter of minutes, if they didn't find a way out, they would literally be inside the snake.

Two white dagger-like pillars fell from the ceiling and crashed into the wooden bookcases between Danny and Theo.

Like fangs.

Walls suddenly formed on either side of the white pillar fangs, just as Stokes streaked in from up high. But Theo's eyes were on the walls forming— pink walls, like a throat, with the chandelier glowing at the back.

It was a throat, it had to be, and Theo was inside it.

Crying out in panic, he spun and sprinted out, just as Stokes landed. Tripping over the Roush, Theo sprawled on the floor and then jumped to his feet.

"I found it!" Stokes said, flapping to his feet. "A gold box, there, in the chandelier."

Danny ran up, panting. "In the chandelier?"

They turned and looked between the fangs, down the snake's throat where the red carpet throbbed like a long tongue. The chandelier hung near the back of the throat.

"The glasses are there?" Danny asked, voice tight.

On queue, a golden box dropped from the glowing red chandelier and landed on a small white platform that had formed at the back of the snake's throat.

The chandelier winked out, plunging the hallway, which Theo was certain was a throat, into darkness. A dull glow came from the golden box—like a lure daring them to come take a bite.

The only way to the glasses was into the snake's dark throat.

"**W**e just have to go back there now and get them," Theo said after a long silence.

"No way," Danny muttered. "Stokes can go."

"Me?"

"You can fly, right? It's dark and the floor is . . . who knows what we'll find in there. It's alive!"

"I would, truly I would," Stokes said, walking over and tapping one of the fangs. He turned back. "But I'm forbidden from retrieving anything for you. I'm only here to guide you and send Shataiki to the pit they came from."

"What?" Danny stammered.

"It's okay," Theo said, taking Danny's arm. "We go together. Remember, fear blinds us. We go in now, straight for the glasses. The sooner we get them on, the sooner we'll find the third seal. The only way out is in."

Danny stared down the dark hallway at the glowing box at the end. Finally, he nodded. "Yes, the only way out is in. And I'm not so bad in the darkness; it's just the thought of this thing being alive around us that freaks me out."

"It wants us to be afraid. We have to go into the darkness. It's the only way to learn how to see in the darkness."

Danny stared at Theo as if something he'd said had special meaning.

"What?" Theo asked.

"What you just said: the only way to learn how to see in darkness is to go into it. That's how blind people learn to see in darkness. We ignore the darkness and learn to see in other ways."

Theo nodded. "The only way to see in the darkness is to get the Kingdom glasses, and those are in there." He jabbed a finger down the hallway. "Down this hallway."

"I think you mean throat."

Theo nodded. "Come on."

Theo tentatively led Danny past the fangs and into the "throat," being careful not to step on the red-carpet tongue. He couldn't shake the feeling that if he stepped on it, they would be swallowed up into the belly of the snake.

He shivered.

Stokes stood at the entrance, watching them with round eyes, keeping guard. If something went wrong, he would try to help, but he couldn't help them retrieve the glasses.

The hallway was damp and cold, with a thick musky smell. But it became quite wider the farther they went in. It was as if the whole library was inside the snake now, with bookshelves rising on the sides, some with actual books, some made of scales. But in the dim light, they couldn't see much more than that.

Theo's feet crunched against the floor. He tried not to think of what could be underneath him. It sounded like dried leaves. Or . . .

Danny paused. "Sounds like we're stepping on bugs. I really don't like bugs."

"Don't look down." Theo picked up his pace. "We just need to reach the glasses. Hurry!"

His foot got caught on something, and he stumbled sideways into the wall. He felt a twinge of pain in his palm and quickly jerked it away.

"Don't touch the wall," he said, shaking goo off his hand.

"Why not?"

"I think it bit me."

"It can't bite you. We're already inside its mouth."

The box that held their freedom began to glow brighter, sending streams of light into the mouth of the serpent.

"No, it can bite. Look!"

The walls moved in a tangled mass of smaller snakes. All different kinds and colors of snakes slithered one atop another.

Behind him, Danny gasped. Theo spun. Danny stood rooted to the floor. Below his feet moved a thick carpet of insects. He'd been right. They were walking on bugs! The insects crawled up and down Danny's pant legs as he began to frantically brush them off.

It was as if the closer they got to the glasses, the worse things got around them.

"Everything okay?" Stokes yelled from the opening of the mouth.

But Theo was too distracted by the wall of snakes to answer him. He watched as one of the larger snakes lifted its body off the wall and lashed out toward him with jaws open. He ducked.

But another snake was peeling itself off the wall, eying Theo—then another and another, dozens, maybe hundreds of them—ready to attack.

"Run!" Theo cried as he dodged another snake.

They ran blindly, desperate to reach safety, only twenty feet away now. Theo reached the square platform, out of breath and nauseous. He threw himself onto its white surface and pulled himself up and free of the snakes, which stopped short at its base.

Danny sprawled to his right, shaken but safe. The snakes and bugs retreated, losing interest in them.

"We made it," Theo panted.

They exchanged a relieved glance and stood to their feet. The glowing box waited at the center.

Theo crossed to the box, dropped to his knees, and brushed his finger on the lid. The warm glow pulsed through his skin.

Danny knelt beside him, breathing hard. "Open it."

Theo held his breath and slowly opened the box. His heart stopped. "There's nothing here. It's empty."

"No glasses? How can that be?"

He reached in and felt the sides and bottom, just to be sure there was no hidden compartment. Nothing. It was all a trick! They'd been lured into the snake's throat and were going to be swallowed alive!

"Wait," Danny said, reaching for something under the box. "What's this?"

Theo pushed the box aside and stared at what it had been sitting on—an old book with a brown leather cover. The word "Truth" was etched into its surface.

He reached for the book. The moment his fingers made contact with the surface, the book glowed hot and bright.

He gasped and withdrew his hand.

On its own, the cover opened. The glowing pages flipped open one by one, until finally stopping.

But suddenly there was more than light. Words penned in a dark ink edged with streaming light began to appear as if written by an invisible hand.

Eight words. That's all, and then the writing stopped.

"What does it say?" Danny asked.

Theo's voice trembled as he read the words aloud. "Behold, the Kingdom of Heaven is within you."

"The Kingdom is inside us? That doesn't make sense. We were just there."

But something about it did make sense. Theo could feel it in his bones.

"The Kingdom of Heaven is you." He turned to Danny. "Justin told us that when we see clearly, we see through the eyes of the Kingdom."

"And the gold-rimmed glasses are the lenses to the Kingdom of Heaven," Danny said. "This is just writing."

Theo stood and paced, lost in thought.

"In the first two rooms we needed the lenses, but not in this last level. Here, the Kingdom is inside us. So how do we see what's inside us?"

"As I said, it doesn't make sense," Danny said, scrambling to his feet. "It's a trap! We have to get out of here!"

The snakes hissed and nipped at the edge of the stage.

Theo held out his hand. "Wait! I don't think so. I think this is the way out!"

A deep hiss emerged from somewhere in the throat, followed by a warm, putrid breeze. Danny backed toward the edge of the stage. The room began to tremble. The snake was reacting to the fact that he was speaking the truth.

Theo glanced up and saw that the ceiling was slowly sinking, like a closing jaw. But they couldn't run. Not now. Not with what he knew.

"This is what I know! One, white: God is the light without darkness. Nothing can threaten him!" His words echoed through the chamber.

The white ring on his shoulder began to grow hot. The first seal was glowing brightly.

"This is what I know!" he said, louder now. "Two, green: We are the light of the world, made of the same light that is our Father. In that light, nothing can threaten us!"

The green circle joined in with its light.

"This is what I know!" Theo continued. "The light is the Kingdom of Heaven and it can only be seen with the eyes of the Kingdom." All the pieces of the puzzle began to fall together in his mind. "But we are blind. We are blind and we need new lenses to see what is *always* here to see—the Kingdom, the light inside us!"

Danny blinked at him. "Blind?"

"All of us, Danny. The whole world is blind to the light inside us. That's the point of this game. You said that being blind forced you to find another way to see. The eyes of the Kingdom are our other way to see! We have to see with the eyes of the Kingdom or we remain blind and in darkness."

"Otherwise we see darkness and fear, which only blind us more," Danny breathed. "That's seeing with the eyes of the world. But—"

The room trembled. Saliva splattered on the stage as the jaw clenched tighter.

Danny stared at Theo. "But with the eyes of the Kingdom, we see light instead of darkness!"

"That has to be it!" Theo cried.

"And the Kingdom is within us."

"Which means we don't need a pair of gold glasses to see it. The glasses are inside of us! We can see with the eyes of the Kingdom that are within us!"

"Look!" Danny jumped up to the book. New words had been etched below the eight Theo had read.

Theo knelt down, ignoring the hot breath, hissing, and signs of doom all around him. He read the words aloud for Danny. "What is your purpose in this life?"

They both stared, wide-eyed.

"It's a clue," Danny said.

"The final clue to the third seal. The third is all about perception, about blindness and sight, about darkness and light, about seeing with the eyes of the Kingdom instead of the eyes of the world."

"Which is why I'm here," Danny said with growing excitement. "I gained sight coming here. We can all gain sight when we see with the eyes of the Kingdom inside of us!"

The hissing became a rasping roar and the walls began to writhe. Theo closed his eyes.

"The first seal was white for light. The second was green for the light in this life. The third . . ."

And then he had it. he was sure. "Black!" he shouted, snapping his eyes open. He faced Danny.

"Black. Darkness. Our quest is to see the light in darkness. We live in darkness to the Kingdom of Heaven, and our quest is to see it! It's our purpose!"

Danny jerked up his own sleeve. Theo watched in amazement as the white seal, then the green seal, and finally the third and black seal appeared on Danny's arm.

Heat burned at Theo's shoulder. The third seal was on his shoulder too.

Danny looked at him. "Wow!"

"Yeah, wow!" Theo echoed.

With a final, gut-wrenching rasp, the foul breath of wind suddenly stopped. The walls and the ceiling disintegrated into a black fog and pulled up toward the ceiling as if someone was sucking it up through a straw.

In a matter of seconds, everything around them simply vanished—the snake, the library, the elaborate stage, all gone.

Theo and Danny found themselves kneeling in the garden, facing Justin. Stokes was bouncing up and down beside him, seemingly barely able to contain his enthusiasm.

Danny jumped up, threw his fist in the air. "We did it!"

Justin chuckled. "I never had a moment's doubt."

"We are the light," Theo said, standing. "But we're

blind to who we are. Our quest is to see the light in the darkness and for that we need to see through the eyes of the Kingdom."

"Exactly," Justin said.

It's all so simple.

The whole world was blind but didn't know it. Whenever someone was in fear, they were in darkness—blind.

"Will I be blind again in my world?" Danny asked, looking up at Justin.

Justin smiled. "In one way, yes. But in a new way, you are beginning to see the way most can't yet see." He placed his hand on Danny's shoulder. "You will be much wiser than many of those who walk around you. Your job now is to help others see like you."

Danny nodded.

Stokes rushed to the boys and hugged them both with his long, floppy wings. "You are brave and wonderful. I love you both!"

"We love you, too, Stokes," Theo said with a laugh.

Stokes pulled away. "You must come back."

"We're leaving now?" Danny asked.

"Yes," Justin said, looking at the horizon. "It is time for you to go home, but we will see you very soon. You still have two seals to find. The fourth seal is the most difficult. When you find it, the fifth will come quickly. In the fifth seal, there is more power

than you can possibly imagine."

Theo didn't think he was ready to go home yet. But then he thought about Annelee waiting in the library. How long had she been there? A whole day had passed here, but from his previous quests, he knew that time wasn't the same in both worlds.

He turned to Danny. "Ready to go home?"

"No," Danny said, surveying the wonder of the garden, using his eyes one last time to see. "But yes."

"Remember who you are," Justin said. He placed two fingers on both boys' foreheads and pushed.

Before Theo could say another word, the world around him faded, leaving him in a peaceful darkness.

Theo opened his eyes and sat up quickly, finding himself in the library once more.

"You're already done?" Annelee asked, shocked. "It's only been, like, two minutes! Why are you already done? Did you get the third seal? Tell me everything! Don't leave out any details! Danny, are you okay?"

"Wow!" Danny said, sitting up with his dark glasses covering his eyes. He lifted up his sleeve and felt the warm, glowing tattoo on his skin. "Wow!"

"The third seal!" she cried. She instinctively reached over to touch her arm. The moment her fingers made contact with her skin, she gasped. Her eyes closed and her mouth hung up. A broad smile filled her face.

Light began to glow under her sleeve, followed by a burst of power that flooded the room.

Danny backed away, but Annelee began to laugh.

She raised her sleeve and looked at the black circle resting inside the white and green circles. "The Kingdom of Heaven! I was wondering how I'd learn about the third seal without going on the quest."

"Now you know what we know," Theo said. "White: Elyon is the light without darkness. He is all powerful and cannot be threatened."

Annelee grabbed Theo by his hand and said, "Green: we are the light of the world but often don't know because we are blind."

She took one of Danny's hands. Theo reached for the other, completing the circle. Danny smiled. "Black: our journey is to see the light in the darkness. When we don't, it's because we're blind, looking through the wrong lenses."

A warm glow flowed around them. Everything felt perfect.

A slow clapping interrupted the reunion.

Theo spun to find Asher standing at the doorway of their hideaway. "Asher!"

"That's right. It's me," he said, stepping into the room. "Sorry to break up your little love fest. Pathetic, but fun to watch."

Asher crept closer, his eyes shadowed by giant, dark circles, and his skin paler than usual. He looked

like he hadn't slept in days. There was something off—more than just a lack of sleep. He stopped in front of them, offering them a blank stare.

That's when Theo saw it: Shax—the sickening Shataiki who'd tormented him on his first quest. It was only a faint outline, but there was no mistaking the beast. The black bat had crossed over and had latched onto Asher's back like a virus, reminding Theo of his fear in the second level.

The Shataiki glared at him and then whispered into Asher's ear. Asher looked over at the table where the book was lying.

"Nice book, Theo," he said, walking over to it. He

ran his fingers over the leather binding of *The Book of History*. "It looks exactly like they said it would."

Theo's mind raced. He wasn't afraid, just confused. How was Shax over here? What was he doing with Asher?

Shax whispered into Asher's ear again. The bully flipped open the book and grinned at Theo. "So you three have been doing some traveling. Place has a lot of power, I hear." He looked back at the book and touched the three bloody finger marks on the blank page. "Danny, Annelee, and Theo. Three marks."

Asher slammed the book closed and picked it up.

"Asher, please listen to us," Theo said.

"Put the book down and leave us alone!" Annelee snapped.

Asher chuckled under his breath. "I think it's time for me to have some of that power, don't you?"

He raced from the room, moving with an inhuman speed.

How is this happening?

They stood in stunned silence. Part of Theo wanted to chase Asher down, but he knew there was no way he could catch him. And with the Shataiki latched to his back, he'd never be able to wrestle the book away from him. Not here. Not at school.

"We have to stop him!" Annelee said, hurrying for the door.

"We can't. Not like this. He's too fast and strong."

She spun back, face white. "He's going to use the book and travel over. You realize that, don't you? That can't be good."

She was right. This had to be part of Shadow Man's plan.

"So anyone can travel through the book?" Danny asked.

"So it seems." Annelee faced Theo. "Well? How are we going to get it back?"

Fear lapped at Theo's mind. He looked at the seals glowing on her arm. Fear was a lie. He would not let it blind him. They had three seals—two more to go.

He took a deep breath and let it out slowly. Then he headed for the door, Shadow Man's promise emerging from memory: "I will win one way or another, boy. Even if it means finding you in your world, I will blind you."

"I don't know how we're going to get the book back," he said. "But without it, the seals we have will soon be gone. And then it will be like all of this never happened."

Annelee stared at him for a long moment.

"Then we'd better figure something out."

"And quickly," Theo said.

CONTINUE THE QUEST!